WHEN WOLVES HOWL

Georgia Graham

Haze crouches low as he steals closer
to the other wolves in his pack. His ears are
back, his tail curled under him. He's a big wolf,
but he never pushes his way to the front.
He doesn't show his teeth or rest his paws on the back of
another wolf. He looks away when the others glare at him.

Haze is the least powerful of all the wolves in his pack.
Only the young pups look up to him.

Night and Snow are Haze's parents. They are the leaders of the pack, the Alpha male and female. They hold their tails high. Their eyes glow. They are father and mother to all the wolves in their pack. This includes the pups born in the spring a few months ago, and also the grown wolves born the spring before.

Stormy, the Beta, ranks next. He is Haze's brother. His eyes shine like twin moons as he learns to hunt from Night. The other grown wolves also lord over Haze. Haze is the Omega wolf, the lowest of the low. Haze is pale gray like the dull winter sun unable to shine.

But Haze is the first one the pups will scramble to play with.

The wolves are hungry now. Night howls to get the pack ready for a hunt. They all join in the chorus. So does Haze, though his voice is low. Night leads his pack with powerful steady strides. Ravens trace their route above the treetops. Night bounds toward a lakeshore where the hoofed ones often gather to drink.

By late afternoon, the pack arrives at the lake. The scent of the grass eaters is faint. The wolves hear no sound of hooves, no call of an injured elk, no cries from lost offspring. The hoofed ones have moved on.

Hunger gnaws at the wolves' bellies. As Night leads them on, Haze follows at the rear of the pack. Further along the lake's edge, they get close to a herd, then slow to a crawl and finally stop.

Upwind, they crouch frozen, ears tall. A herd of mountain sheep nibble shrubs. The sheep start to leave. Night studies the herd, looking for a very young sheep, or a very old one, or one with an uneven gait. Soon, he sees one that is limping. All the wolves surround the sheep, chase it, and bring it down. It is a quick kill.

The wolves begin devouring the meat they need to survive. The ravens soon appear at the kill. They flutter up and down, snatching their own morsels from the carcass.

Haze carefully creeps up. The other wolves snarl and snap at him. He rolls over on his back. But as their bellies fill, Haze inches up again and joins in. Soon, they are all gorging, swallowing whole chunks along with pieces of the hide.

Bellies full, the hunters head back home. Snow waits with her pups. The wolves leap
when they see the three little ones yelping, their blue eyes sparkling. The pups lick
at the wolves' mouths, demanding to be fed. The hunters regurgitate soft
warm sheep stew into the pups' open mouths. Night rewards
Snow with a generous helping.

The wolves bask in the summer sun. The pups climb all over Haze, tugging at his ears and swatting his tail. He tumbles and plays with them gently.

The wolves are full and can rest now. They spend several days sleeping and relaxing.

Haze's three brothers stand over him and rumble a deep growl. Haze crouches low and meekly licks Stormy's muzzle. Then he rolls out from them and starts a game of chase. Before long all the wolves are wrestling, tugging at sticks, and playing king-of-the-hill.

The wolves howl long into the light of the late summer evening.

Then, they hear the howls of a rival pack of wolves in the neighboring forest. They have been trespassing into Night's forest and marking the tree trunks with their urine. Night's pack howls back, warning them to stay away.

With Haze singing bass, they howl in harmony. With many different yips and yowls, it sounds as if there are more in their pack than there really are. Their chorus echoes off the mountains and trails down the valleys.

It has been over a week since their last kill and the wolves' bellies are
feeling the gnaw of hunger again. The pups whine. The pack howls.
It is time for another hunt. Now Snow is pacing, ready to lead the
hunt with Night. Haze sits with the pups. The three young ones lean
into their favorite older brother as the rest of the pack sets off.

Haze waits with the pups all day, as the
sun moves across the sky.

   Suddenly, he straightens up, tense and
stiff, his ears aimed toward the rival wolf
pack that is coming closer. Haze noses the
frightened little ones under a fallen log and
paces nervously. Now the outsiders bound
toward Haze and the pups.

When they arrive, Haze leaps into their path and leads them away from the pups. They chase after him, nipping at his heels. One wolf slams into him, and the others trample him. Then they hear the approaching howls of Night's pack and disappear into the dark. Haze lies beaten and battered in the forest.

Night, Snow, and the others soon come back from the hunt. They find the terrified pups in their hiding place. Then they stalk around uneasily, sniffing for Haze.

Before long, Snow lets out a yelp in the forest. Night joins her. Haze is lying there, his eyes closed. Snow licks his forehead. Haze lifts one eyelid and wags his tail but he cannot get up. The other wolves curl up by Haze.

In the days that follow, each time the wolves hunt and return to feed the pups, they feed Haze as well. And soon he is strong again.

Now, Haze does not crouch or look away in fear of the other wolves. Ears forward, tail high, he is no longer the Omega. That role has shifted to another wolf.

This time, when the
pack howls, the deep voice
of Haze is stronger. And
the pups sing in harmony
with their favorite big
brother.

Text and illustration copyright © 2018 Georgia Graham

Published in Canada by Red Deer Press
195 Allstate Parkway, Markham, ON   L3R 4T8

Published in the United States by Red Deer Press
311 Washington Street, Brighton, MA   02135

Red Deer Press acknowledges with thanks the Canada Council for the Arts and the Ontario Arts C ouncil for their support of our publishing program. We acknowledge the financial support of the Government of Canada through the Canada Book Fund (CBF) for our publishing activities.

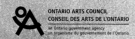 

Edited for the Press by Peter Carver
Design by Brooke Kerrigan
Printed in China by Sheck Wah Tong Printing Press Ltd.
www.reddeerpress.com

Library and Archives Canada Cataloguing in Publication
Graham, Georgia, 1959-, author, illustrator
When wolves howl / Georgia Graham.
ISBN 978-0-88995-518-9 (hardcover)
I. Title.
PS8563.R33W43 2018   jC813'.54   C2018-900432-0

Publisher Cataloging-in-Publication Data (U.S.)
Names: Graham, Georgia, author, illustrator.
Title: When Wolves Howl / written & illustrated by Georgia Graham.
Description: Markham, Ontario : Red Deer Press, 2018. | Summary: "Life in a wolf pack is vividly explored in this colorful adventure picture book showcasing animals in their natural environment, cubs, family life, competition in forest and mountain and the daily survival of wolves" – Provided by publisher.
Identifiers: ISBN 978-0-88995-518-9 (hardcover)
Subjects: LCSH: Wolves – Juvenile fiction. | Wolves -- Behavior – Juvenile fiction. | BISAC: JUVENILE FICTION / Animals / Wolves & Coyotes. | JUVENILE FICTION / Nature & the Natural World / General.
Classification: LCC PZ7.G734Wo |DDC [F] – dc23

To the wolves,
   May the myths about you end. May your true
      beauty and love for each other shine through.

—G.G